HERE THEY COME. THERE THEY GO.

What Ben Didn't Know...

Andy Labis

Webventure Publishing

The characters and events portrayed in this book are fictitious. Any similarity to real persons, living or dead, is coincidental and not intended by the author.

ISBN E-Book: 979-8-9945082-5-1
ISBN Paperback: 979-8-9945082-6-8

Cover Design by: Andy Labis

For the young boys who want to eat like their dads.

CONTENTS

A SPECIAL OCCASION

While sitting at the dining room table over dinner, Ben asked Amy, "Honey, why don't we enjoy the trip into the city for our anniversary? Let someone else drive for a change."

"I don't know, it might be nice to relax, but I hate to spend the money," replied Amy.

As their night out was on the horizon, Ben understood Amy's reasoning but pressed on, "Yea, but it's our anniversary. This way we can share a bottle of wine and not have to worry about driving."

"I don't know, sometimes I worry about what kind of driver we are going to get, especially having to travel that far. It's not like we can just jump out of the car if they aren't that good," said a worried Amy.

Ben thought back to a time he took the train into the city for work and hired a ride-share for a short trip from the train station to the office. He remembered the horrible driver he had, but still replied to Amy, doing his best to reassure her, "It will be fine. We'll make sure we get one with a good rating, even spring for the luxury ride so we are in a nicer car and not something like this gold jalopy I was in this one time."

"That's still a lot of money," Amy replied, resigned to the fact Ben wasn't going to let this suggestion go.

As Ben gave a look of "Please," Amy caved, "Oh, alright. It might be nice to just sit in the back seat with you and enjoy the ride."

Ben grinned with a look of satisfaction that they would hire a car. He also wasn't sure what excited him more, just being able to relax on the drive with Amy, or that he could brag to his family how they took a car into the city for their anniversary dinner.

"Don't worry, honey," proclaimed Ben. "I'll take care of it! It will be great!"

As much as Ben put on a face of confidence, inside he was a little worried about the driver. He hoped by getting the luxury ride that things would be better, and maybe the driver wouldn't even talk to them.

"By the way, where are we going for dinner?" asked Ben.

"I thought you set up dinner?" said Amy, with a grin.

Ben looked flustered, knowing Amy always does better finding a great restaurant.

"Don't worry," Amy said with a chuckle, "I took care of it. We're going to The Marbled Fin. You can get a giant steak, and I read they have a fantastic Chilean Sea Bass for me."

Ben reached over the table and held Amy's hand.

"I love you so much," said Ben, with gratitude in his voice for not having to find a restaurant.

Amy looked at him with a smile, "Ditto."

THE STEAK BUFFET

Ben always loved what he called "the fancy dinners" in the city, especially when he would think back to his childhood. His family wasn't poor, but they didn't have that much, either, and the town they lived in didn't have what most would consider upscale dining.

The great restaurants near Ben were about a 40 minute drive away. He would think how, when he was growing up, that 40-minute drive seemed like an eternity, but nowadays, the same amount of time feels like a short trip.

For Ben when he was growing up, "fancy dinner" meant The Steak Buffet, and going there happened maybe once a year. Ben could recollect the trips, one town over, just past his Aunt's house. He remembered the restaurant, a collection of booths and tables, and a western motif with decorations that looked like they came from a second-hand store in Arizona.

He recalled that it wasn't fancy dining as there wasn't a host or hostess to seat you at a table, but rather you would enter through the swinging doors painted to look like they were from an old-time saloon and follow the hallway to a buffet line. He could see his small hands taking a red, plastic tray from a stack of them at the front of the buffet and sliding it down the metal rails. Barely able to see over the rails, he could just see the trays of various food as he would peer through the glass.

The line always started with rolls and butter, with his mom helping him by grabbing the tongs and putting a roll on his plate. As he walked down the line, Ben had his gaze trained on the very end, where the steak was resting in metal serving trays. Along the way were all of the food groups Ben didn't like, soggy green beans, mashed potatoes, and carrots that looked to be soaked in a vat of butter and water.

He would see his dad get served the mashed potatoes, and then confidently say to the server stationed behind the counter, "I'll have some mashed potatoes, please," trying to be like his dad. Ben didn't really want them, but he was eating like a "grown-up." As the server handed Ben a bowl of mashed potatoes, he always wondered why they never had tiny potato chunks in them, like his mom would make.

Finally came the main dishes. There was generally a hodge-podge of entrees, usually a mix of trays that would contain questionable fish sitting in puddles of butter, fried chicken that looked as if it had been under heat lamps for hours, and there, at the end of the line, the T-bone steak. Before the steak, however, was always meatloaf, smothered in catsup, with the top of the catsup looking crusty as the heat lamps sucked any moisture out of the one thing that would make the meatloaf palatable.

As Ben would walk down the line, he would see his dad say, "I'll have one of those T-bones, and make sure it's dead!"

Ben didn't know what that meant at the time, but over the years he came to learn it meant well-done.

Ben, though, didn't care about how the steak was cooked; he just wanted to eat like his dad.

As he would slide his tray with anticipation, just as he was about to pass the meatloaf, every time from behind him his mom would say, "Benny will have a piece of meatloaf," pointing to the server behind the counter who would dish a slab of meatloaf, that by this time looked a little like a dried hockey puck slathered with dehydrated catsup, onto Ben's plate.

"But, Mom, I wanted a steak like dad got!" Ben would complain.

"When you get a job you can have a steak. Today you get meatloaf," his mom would respond.

Ben's dad looked back at him, as if to say, "If it were up to me, I'd let you have a steak," but then would agree with Ben's mom, "Someday, son, you'll get a steak. Today, enjoy the great meatloaf."

Finally past the buffet line and to their table, Ben would try to enjoy his meatloaf, but mostly kept looking at his dad enjoying the gray T-bone. A smile would come to his face as his dad would always cut off a few little pieces and slip them on Ben's plate. Stabbing a piece with his fork like he needed to kill it, Ben would put it in his mouth wondering why it tasted like leather.

"Ben, here, have some of this steak sauce," his dad would mention as he noticed the look on Ben's face. "Just smother it on there."

Ben wondered, if the steak were so delicious, why did it need sauce? Instead of questioning the tastiness of the steak, however, he would smother steak sauce on the remaining pieces and pretend to enjoy them.

From those days forward Ben always dreamed of having a great steak, from a real steakhouse, without steak sauce.

A NIGHT OUT

Ben had been looking forward to this day for weeks, dreaming of the steak and a wonderful night with Amy. As the day was coming up, he was slightly concerned what kind of driver he would end up with. He kept replaying his bad experience with a driver on the way to work, but felt more confident things would be better this time since they were getting the nicer car.

Finally the day came, Ben ordered the car, proudly selecting "Ride in Style." A couple of options came up, one car was five minutes away and the driver was rated 4.7 out of 5, another was thirty minutes away rated 4.9, and another right around the corner at 4.3.

Ben thought, "Gosh, thirty minutes for the best rated ride. That worries me, what if traffic is bad or gets lousy on the way to the restaurant? I don't want to be late. They might not hold the reservation. But 4.7, I remember selecting someone with a 4.7 before and that was a nightmare."

"Honey, do you think someone rated 4.7 will be good enough for us?" Ben asked Amy, in his head thinking if the ride was bad, then it was her choice.

"What," yelled Amy from the bathroom, finishing up.

Ben yelled a little louder, "Do you think a driver rated 4.7 will be good enough? He's only five minutes away."

Amy, with a slight annoyance in her voice, replied, "I'm sure it will be fine."

Ben selected the driver rated at 4.7, and a window popped

up on his screen, “Santiago will arrive in about five minutes. They will be driving a black sedan, ready to take you to your destination.”

Ben noticed the profile button for Santiago and pressed it. A bubble opened up on his screen, “Hello, I’m Santiago! I’m originally from a small town in Chile. I’m looking forward to giving you a wonderful ride! You should find water in the back seat should you want some. Feel free to let me know, when you get in the car, if you prefer conversation or would rather keep the conversation to a minimum. I’m here to make your trip as enjoyable as possible!”

Ben thought, “Geez, that’s such a relief. I wonder if it is rude, though, to tell him I don’t really want to talk?”

Ben was looking at the map on the screen and noticed that the car was coming around the corner to pick them up.

Without looking away from his screen, Ben hollered, “Honey, the car is almost here. Are you almost ready?” oblivious to the fact Amy was right behind him.

Amy yelled back, directly over Ben’s shoulder and into his ear, “Yes, dear, I’m ready!”

Startled, Ben turned around. Amy hit Ben with a “Gotcha!” smile, chuckling at Ben’s being absorbed at the image of the car traveling on his phone screen.

For a split second Ben was annoyed, but that quickly shifted to noticing how beautiful Amy was. All he knew now was how much he was looking forward to a wonderful night with her in the city.

“The car should be here any second,” Ben mentioned. “The driver’s name is Santiago, he’s from Chile.”

“How do you know?” inquired Amy.

“I read his profile. This should be a great ride. You can tell him not to talk to you,” mentioned Ben.

Amy questioned Ben's bringing up talking with the driver, "Why would anyone do that?"

"The last time I had a driver who wouldn't stop talking. This way we can just enjoy the ride together," Ben replied.

"Let's just see how it goes. Okay, Honey?" Amy mentioned with a calm voice.

"Okay," Ben answered, "It looks like the car is here. Let's go."

Ben and Amy walked out the front door, Ben skipping a little bit to the car much to the wonderment of Amy.

As they got to the car, Santiago had already gotten out to let Amy in the rear door. Ben smiled knowing this would be a great ride.

DRIVING TO THE CITY

As Ben and Amy fastened their seatbelts, Santiago asked Ben, "I'm assuming you are Ben?"

"Yes, you must be Santiago?"

Santiago, with cheerfulness in his voice, responded, "That I am! I see you are heading into the city, going to The Marbled Fin. Would you like any conversation along the way, or would you prefer I keep things to a minimum?"

Ben felt this giant sense of relief, simply commenting, "Let's play it by ear."

"That sounds wonderful," quipped Santiago.

Santiago backed the car out of the driveway and started down the street. Before he could get to the end of the block, Ben jokingly asked, in his favorite bad dad-joke voice, "Your profile mentioned you were from Chile. Was it cold in the town you grew up in?"

Ben chuckled as if he were being exceptionally funny, and Amy groaned wondering if the hour in the car was going to be filled with Ben and bad jokes.

Santiago chuckled, as if to humor Ben, then replied, "I originally come from a small village name Puerto Natales. It can get quite cool there, though not as cold as some of the winters I have been through here in Chicago."

Ben took a pause, wondering what to say next.

"How did you end up in Chicago from all the way in Chile?" Ben asked.

"I came here for university. I have an uncle who is a doctor in Chicago. He grew up in Chile but studied in Chicago. As I was graduating school he came to visit, and told me that I should come here. There would be many more opportunities for me here than in Puerto Natales," explained Santiago.

In Ben's head came the thought, "What have I done? I'm horrible at a conversation. Why did I ask him that? Now he's going to think I want to talk the entire trip. It would be rude to ask him not to talk anymore. Dang it."

"When did you come here?" was all Ben could come up with at the time.

"I got here seven years ago," Santiago replied, with an apprehension in his voice not knowing if he should try to continue the conversation or let it die.

"Do you like it in Chicago?" Ben asked, awkwardly trying to carry on the conversation.

"Yes," answered Santiago, "It is so much different than my village. So many things to do. So exciting."

"How long have you been driving for the company?" was all Ben could come up with next.

"I've been driving for two years now, after I graduated," Santiago replied, still unsure how much to add.

Ben, at a complete loss of what to ask next, started to look out the window, but Amy, hearing the initial conversation, became curious about Santiago. She wondered how someone would find their way from a small town in Chile up to Chicago.

"That's fascinating. I know you mentioned your uncle was a doctor. What kind of doctor is he?" Amy inquired.

Santiago felt that there was an ease in the way Amy asked him the question, as if she was really curious and not just trying to have small talk.

"He is an ear, nose, and throat surgeon. I think they call them

E.N.T.'s here in the United States? He came to the United States twenty years ago for medical school and never left. It took him a long time to become a citizen here, but felt it was worth every struggle. He really loves it here."

"That does seem like a long way, from Chile to Chicago. What did you study?" Amy asked, leaning a little closer to the front seat so she could hear Santiago better.

Santiago explained, "I came to go to medical school, like my uncle, but really didn't like it after a couple of years. There was a lot more studying which I wasn't used to, coming from my school, and I really didn't like having to cut into people. I really came here hoping to eventually be able to afford to bring my parents and brother up here, but so far that hasn't worked out."

"Now I'm dreaming of being a writer," finished Santiago.

Amy leaned forward a little more, with total interest in everything Santiago was saying. Meanwhile, Ben was looking out the window as the car sped down the highway, half-listening to the conversation, hoping that he could somehow find a great question to ask.

Ben chimed in, "I find looking at that stuff, you know, up noses and stuff, kind of cool. I saw some videos on the internet, and it was like looking into another world up there."

"I don't know, being a doctor always sounded cool to me," Ben mentioned quietly, acknowledging the awkwardness, and finished up his thought with, "Being a writer, though, gosh, I think I could do that, too."

Both Santiago and Amy nicely, at the same time, made a sound acknowledging what Ben had said, but both wondered how it fit into the conversation.

What Ben didn't know was that Santiago had been writing his

entire life.

SANTIAGO

As Amy asked, "Where is, what you said, 'Puerto Natales,' down in Chile?" Santiago's thoughts drifted back to his childhood.

"It's a little town by Patagonia. It's a tourist town, mostly, as people would make their way to Patagonia."

"You must have met a lot of people down there?" Amy inquired. "I had a friend who went to Patagonia and said it was beautiful. They might have even come through your town."

Santiago thought back to his time in the small village of Puerto Natales and began talking:

"I always remembered seeing tourists on their way to Patagonia. Growing up, my parents insisted that I learn English. They wanted someone to be able to talk to the tourists so they could sell their hats, scarves, and gloves that my mother knitted.

"They were the warmest items, made from the wool of the sheep of a nearby rancher. My mother had a little stand on the corner of the street, but she only knew the local Spanish and didn't want to learn English. It was hard for her to try and sell things.

"The tourists used to call me "cute little boy," and were always surprised when I spoke English. I was told that they would tell their friends at the hotels to get a hat from the "cute little boy."

"I didn't mind, it helped money come in. I would yell at the corner, "Warm hats! You're going to need them!

"I was also really good at, what is that called, upselling? They would come to buy the hat their friend told them to buy, and I would get them to buy a scarf and gloves. I kind of felt bad because the gloves weren't that great. If they would get wet your hands would freeze, but it was fun getting their money, and they all smiled when they put them on saying they really felt warm, and the wool was so soft.

"'Better than alpaca,' I always told them, but I didn't know if that was true. I just knew they seemed to know what an alpaca was, so it sounded good."

Santiago caught a glance of Ben, looking out the window, not really paying attention.

"I'm sorry, I talk too much. I can stop if you'd like."

"No, your story is fascinating," said Amy. "I love hearing how people end up where they are."

"Okay," said Santiago, "I don't know why, I guess because I could speak English, but many of the tourists would tell me things, of their trips, and I would ask them where they were from, what they did, and where they were going. Many of the people would say how they just needed to get away from their 'daily grind,' and thought Patagonia would be a fun adventure. I don't know, didn't seem like an adventure to me.

"At night I would write down their stories the best I could remember, but I usually forgot most of the stuff they told me so I made up a lot of it in my notebook.

"I always loved talking to the tourists and writing down their stories, but I remember my mother and father always talking about my uncle, how he left our village to go to North America. They called him a "brain doctor," but he never did anything with brains, just the stuff around it. They always talked about how he made more money than they could dream of.

"Back then I dreamed of being a 'brain doctor.' I felt bad for how my mother had to knit all the scarves and hats and gloves, and thought that if I could be a doctor, I could take them to the excitement of North America, and she wouldn't have to knit any more.

"I think I was around fourteen years old when my uncle came to visit. I was old enough to see how my family was mesmerized by him. I remember he seemed like the smartest person I had ever met. He had this big, gold watch, showing up at our little house in a car driven by a chauffeur, like the tourists. It was so cool to me.

"He told me stories of Chicago, how the buildings were as tall as the mountains, and all I thought about during my classes at Enseñanza media, that is what we called what you call high school, was how much I wanted to be a doctor and move to Chicago. I kept helping my mother sell her things, but it got harder for me to be the "cute little boy" as I grew up.

"I still talked to people a lot, and kept writing down their stories."

Amy was mesmerized by Santiago's story about growing up, "I know you mentioned your uncle, and don't take this wrong, but it doesn't seem like it would be easy for you to get to Chicago?"

Santiago continued:

"When I was seventeen, my uncle came back to visit. I was studying science, and at dinner my mother was telling him how good of a student I was. I didn't think I was that smart because we are a small town, even though I was the top of my class, but my mother couldn't stop talking about me.

"My uncle never really cared about me when I was small, but on that trip he seemed to be interested in what I was doing. It was like he realized I wasn't a little boy any more, and I was almost an adult.

"I remember one of the nights he was there. My parents went

to bed, and we were sitting in our living room. He asked me what I planned on doing, and if all I was going to do was keep selling hats and scarves for my family. I told him that I wanted to be a doctor someday, maybe even have enough money so that I could get my parents out of Puerto Natales and to America. That they could probably have a nicer life there.

"He started asking me about school, if I was really doing as well as my mother said, and seemed to care what I was going to do with my life.

"I guess he saw something in me.

"When he was leaving he told me that, if I wanted, he could put in a good word where he went to university in Chicago, that I might be able to get a scholarship.

"I was so excited that night that I couldn't sleep," finished Santiago.

DEAD BODIES

"Gosh," said Amy, "That must have seemed exciting!"

Santiago continued:

"Yes. He helped me get a scholarship, and I felt so bad for my mother because I wouldn't be there to help her any more. She didn't know my plan, to make enough money for them to move, but in my head, I had it all figured out.

"Then I got here. I was okay in university, but it was so much harder. I thought I was smart where I lived, but soon learned I wasn't that smart.

"I mean, I wasn't the worst, but it was so hard. I also remember that first time they showed us a dead body. One of those cadavers, and they made us cut into it. I was so scared. I didn't want to hurt it. I know that sounds weird. It was a dead person, but I hated it.

"I'm sorry, I shouldn't be telling you all of this, you must be celebrating something if you are going to The Marbled Fin," ended Santiago.

By this time Ben had shifted from looking out the window to paying attention to Santiago's story.

"No, this is a great story. We're just going out to dinner. Usually people talk to me about boring stuff, but your story is fascinating. School sounded like a challenge?" Ben said with a sense of "tell me more."

Amy realized Ben was now totally wrapped up in the conversation, and they both looked towards the front seat in anticipation of what Santiago was going to say next.

"Okay, where was I? Oh yeah, dead bodies," started Santiago.

Santiago continued with his story while Ben and Amy listened intently from the back seat.

"The thing was, they only showed us dead bodies the one time. I guess once you get to medical school you have to see them and work on them all of the time. The older students would tell us they made us cut them at the beginning just to scare us, to see if we really wanted to be a doctor. From that moment, though, I started to think that I wouldn't want to be a doctor.

"I didn't want to disappoint my uncle, though. I studied as hard as I could, but the teaching was so much different from my school, and there were so many people in a room. The professor would be up front, writing on this giant board, and I tried to keep up with him. Most of the other kids had computers, but I couldn't afford one, and I didn't want to tell my uncle I needed one because he had already done so much. He probably would have thought me dumb because I remember him telling us stories how he had notebooks and notebooks of lessons when he was in university.

"Even though, I did okay, at least for a normal student, but not for the people who really wanted to be doctors. I would try to study with them, and it never really worked out. For some reason, though, they would talk to me.

"I remember Bill in my class. He was so smart, from Los Angeles. He didn't want to be a doctor at all, but his parents were making him go to school. He wanted to be an actor. I guess that makes sense since he was from Los Angeles, but I wondered why he didn't just tell his parents. Of course I should talk; I didn't want to tell my uncle, either.

"They would all tell me their stories, how they ended up in Chicago, what their parents did, if they had a dog. I didn't get why they would talk to me, but I liked to listen, and would ask a question to keep them going because their stories were so much more interesting to me than learning math and chemistry.

"I would get back to my dorm room at night, and instead of studying I would write their stories in my notebook. I would get to tests and be tired, but somehow I still managed B's and a few A's.

"At first my uncle wasn't that worried with my grades. He always encouraged me, and told me that he knew I could do it. He said that I was having trouble because it was just an adjustment, but I wouldn't tell him that I didn't like it, and that I liked listening to people and writing their stories.

"After the second semester I was still doing okay, but I could tell my uncle thought I should be doing better. He urged me to take some classes in the summer, to "catch up" as he would say, but I really just wanted to go home. I didn't see my parents all year. He said he would pay for a quick trip home and for my summer classes, so I told him I would do it," finished Santiago.

NO MORE DEAD BODIES

Ben struggled with anything to say during the slight break in Santiago's story, mostly mesmerized and wondering how Santiago could pay such great attention to his driving while talking. Amy, though, chimed in, "What was it like going home for only a quick trip?"

Santiago seemed happy to continue, "I remember getting home, and my parents were so proud. But I was afraid because I started to think that I couldn't get good enough grades to be a doctor, and that I couldn't pay for them to come to Chicago to live. I was only home for three weeks. I started to help my mother selling scarves and hats again, but she didn't like it saying, 'That's not work for a doctor!' I started crying to her, telling her I didn't think I could be a doctor. She could see I was afraid that I was letting them down.

"After helping her that day, she stayed up with me after my father went to bed, and we talked. I told her I was scared, that I didn't want to let them down, and about having to cut into the dead body. She was so nice and told me that if I didn't want to be a doctor that it was okay. She also said that maybe I was just having trouble adjusting, and I should give it one more try. If it didn't work, I could come back home.

"I told her I would try, and that I started to love Chicago, and after being home for two weeks I had nothing to do. So I came back for summer school. I did better, and my uncle was happy, so I got to my second year. I had the same troubles with classes as before, but some of my friends figured out a way to hang out with some guys who had graduated and were in medical school, so I hung around with them. The medical students started telling me their stories, how they got to university, and what they were doing in their studies.

"Listening to them, I knew there was no way I could make it, and I wouldn't like it, either. After my next report card, I had to show my grades to my uncle. I could see in his eyes that he knew I wouldn't be a doctor. I almost cried in front of him, but I didn't. He told me how he should have asked me more what I liked to do instead of what I thought I should do.

"He was so supportive, though, and told me that I should at least try to finish university. That if I had a degree I could do anything I wanted. I couldn't believe he said that. He also said that while I was in university he would help find a lawyer to help me get my citizenship if I wanted. So I kept studying in class and tried to become a citizen."

Amy interrupted, "Wow, that's unbelievable. How are things going trying to get your citizenship?"

"Well," Santiago continued, "There is a lot of, what do you call it, red tape? My lawyer says it will just take time, and that I need to keep working, but I really love it here."

"You said you graduated. What did you end up getting a degree in?" asked Amy.

"Well, after telling my uncle, he worked with me to shift my studies to political science. I did find it more interesting, but even while taking the classes, I wondered what kind of job I could get. I was also sad because I knew I wouldn't be able to have my dream of paying for my parents to move. It did keep me in university, though, and that meant people would keep telling me their stories, and I could write them down. I did much better in those classes, graduating with honors, but I didn't know what to do with my degree, and I needed a job. My uncle found a friend who hired me in his office and that somehow lets me stay in the United States, but it's a lonely job doing research. I got this job so I could meet people, and they could tell me their stories.

"Like this one time, I had a guy who I thought must have been a basketball player because his head nearly touched my ceiling. Turned out he told me he was an actor. I didn't know; I don't watch TV or see movies. I asked him what movie he was in, and he said something like "Crashing Weddings" or something.

Amy exclaimed, "I can't believe you had him in your car. I love him! What was he like?"

"He was a really nice guy. He told me he was visiting family. Left me a good tip. There was this other guy, though, he's the reason I ask people if they want conversation when they get in because he gave me a bad review writing, "He talked too much." I guess I do like to talk sometimes, but I'll only do it now if people say it's okay. Usually I don't talk about my life, though, usually I try to find out things about them. Gosh, this drive is so much different. Usually my passengers are telling me their stories, but here I am, just telling you my whole life story."

"Your story is wonderful, Santiago," mentioned Amy. "It's inspiring how you are doing what you can to stay here. Besides, you wouldn't want to listen to my husband's story, he's an accountant."

"Hey," exclaimed Ben, "My job is very exciting!"

Santiago caught Amy's glance in the rearview mirror, and they both seemed to acknowledge that Ben's job was anything but exciting.

"I'm sorry if I'm getting personal, but it doesn't sound like you want to be in that office, and you don't seem like you really want to drive all of the time? You mentioned being a writer?"

Santiago smiled, and with excitement in his voice said, "I want to be a writer, like Studs Terkel. He wrote this great book called "Working," interviewing people. I know I could do something like that."

"That's a wonderful idea," mentioned Amy.

"I actually started writing a story. I'm going to call it "Here They Come. There They Go." It's stories about people's travels," replied Santiago to Amy.

"That sounds fascinating! You really should. I look forward to seeing it as a best seller someday," Amy said with encouragement.

Ben jumped back into the conversation, "I'm thinking of writing a story called, 'The Spreadsheet of Doom.'"

Santiago politely chuckled, and Ben went back to looking out the window starting to think, "Hmm, The Spreadsheet of Doom? I'll bet I could make that a best seller."

NO MEATLOAF

Amy's conversation with Santiago helped the time pass quickly, and as Santiago pulled up to The Marbled Fin, he said with exuberance, "Here we are! I hope you enjoyed the ride!"

Amy replied, "It was wonderful. Best of luck with your writing. I'll be looking for your story."

Ben climbed out of the car, "Thanks. Good luck."

Amy and Ben entered The Marbled Fin and were seated at their table. The restaurant was elegant, a perfect spot for a romantic, anniversary dinner. It was the kind of place Ben could only dream about when he was growing up, a real steakhouse.

Ben grabbed the wine list, intent on trying to find a nice bottle of wine, but all he could do was jokingly, yet secretly meaning it, suggest they get the $400 bottle. "It is our anniversary after all, Honey?"

"Let's just ask the server what a decent bottle of wine would be to go along with our meal," replied Amy in a voice that told Ben this would not be the night for a $400 bottle of wine.

"I'll bet that bottle of wine goes with anything!" Ben exclaimed, trying to be funny. "I know you'll probably be having the Sea Bass, right honey? Hey, that's Chilean Sea Bass. I'll bet our driver was able to get it for next to nothing."

Amy rolled her eyes and said to Ben, "He seemed like a really nice guy. He could probably talk for days about all of the people he has met, and customers he has driven. And the fact that he came from Chile to Chicago, thinking he wanted to be a doctor. That's crazy!"

"Didn't he say something about living in Patagonia. Wonder if he had their jacket, too?" questioned Ben.

"No, he lived in Puerto Natales, near Patagonia, and the tourists would go through his town. You weren't really listening even though you started the conversation, were you?" asked Amy.

"You know me, I'm a great listener," said Ben.

"No, honey, you've perfected the art of pretending to listen to people," commented Amy.

"Ha, ha," said Ben, "Let me check the menu again for what to get."

He thought back to when he was young, and his mom saying, "When you get a job you can have a steak, today you get meatloaf." Ben immediately narrowed in on the 24oz porterhouse steak, although the price of $150 made Ben nervous to tell Amy his choice.

Amy knew exactly what Ben was looking at and sweetly said, "Honey, get the porterhouse. It's our anniversary."

Ben smiled, looking at Amy and commented with every bit of gratitude in his body, "I love you."

A SPREADSHEET DELETED

Ben was sitting in his office at home looking out the window for a spell, as the rain was coming down. He turned back to his computer trying to figure out something to do to kill some time before he and Amy would be going out to dinner. It had been a year since their trip to The Marbled Fin, and Ben still dreamed of the steak he had that night, cooked to perfection, with no hint of steak sauce anywhere to be found.

Looking at his computer, he decided something painless to do would be to clean up some old folders.

"Why the heck did I create something called 'Holding Folder?'" Ben asked himself.

As he double-clicked on the folder, a window slid open revealing a myriad of files and a few folders. Ben started scanning down the list of files. He spotted the self-help guide he downloaded months ago, "How to Get Your Computer Organized for Life." He noticed a copy of the statement from the electric company that he needed when he updated his driver's license. Ben selected those, and a bunch of other files, and moved them to the trash can at the bottom of his screen.

Then he spotted a folder with the title, "Forest Pics." He double-clicked on it, revealing half a dozen pictures he remembered saving from a trip to the local arboretum.

"I've got to remember these are in here," he thought, "I should get them framed someday."

Ben continued selecting files and dragging them down to the trash can. "The World's Best Meatloaf," "blender-manual," "writing templates," "the only guide to the gym you'll ever need," and "brownie recipe" all were transported to the trash.

Then he noticed the folder at the bottom of the list. Ben flashed back to a year earlier when they got home from dinner.

"Honey, you go to bed. I'm going to do a few things in my office," Ben recalled.

"What are you going to do?" Amy asked.

"I've got something I want to work on," Ben replied.

He remembered downloading a writing program onto his computer, selecting the option to "write a novel," saving the folder, and started to write, only to wake up a few hours later face down on his keyboard.

The folder was titled, "The Spreadsheet of Doom."

Ben heard Amy exclaim from the other room, "Oh my God, he did it!" which snapped Ben back into the present moment.

Ben yelled back, "Did what?"

Amy came walking in showing Ben her social media feed, "Here, look at this," she said while handing Ben her phone.

Ben looked at the story on the screen, "Albert's Bookstore welcomes Santiago Concha, bestselling author who will be signing his book, 'Here They Come. There They Go.'"

"Was that our driver from a year ago?" asked Ben.

"It was!" said Amy excitedly. "He wrote his book!"

Ben grunted, "Huh," as he gave Amy back her phone. Then he selected the folder "The Spreadsheet of Doom" and dragged it down to the trash can.

Meanwhile, at Albert's Bookstore in Chicago, Santiago finished up his book signing and walked to the restaurant next door for a party being thrown by his agent. He walked through the door seeing his uncle beaming with pride, and to his surprise his mother and father had flown in from Puerto Natales. He started to cry under the banner that read, “Congratulations to Santiago, New York Times Bestseller! Here They Come. There They Go."

* * *

The End

CONNECTING

To stay connected to Ben and his adventures:
www.whatbendidntknow.com

To stay connected with the author, Andy:
www.allthingsandy.com

For images from Ben's adventures:
www.imagebyandy.store/collections/ben

BOOKS BY THIS AUTHOR

Just Another Lunchtime Walk

Ben feels the need to get out of the workplace during his lunch break, and when the weather is nice, he likes to take a walk in a nearby park. As fate would have it, on this day, Laura, who lives near the park, decides to go for a walk at the same time Ben is finishing up his lunchtime walk.

The Coffee Journey

As summer fades into autumn's gray embrace, Ben discovers a new sanctuary for his lunch breaks: a cozy local coffee shop. But today, he's running late.

Miranda, a college student, finds herself at the same café earlier than usual, seeking a break from her studies.

When an unexpected delay in Ben's order leads to a simple act of kindness, it sets off a chain reaction that touches Miranda's life in a way she couldn't have anticipated.

The Driver

Ben's commute to his downtown office takes an unexpected turn. After a commuter train ride, he is forced to use a ride-sharing service due to unexpected rain and a forgotten umbrella.

His driver, Richard, proves to be more than Ben bargained for, filling the journey with uncomfortable conversation and a few close calls on the road.

The Polish Donut

On Fat Tuesday, Ben's love for paczki turns a simple bakery trip with his wife Amy into something unexpected. When a stranger ahead of them forgets his wallet, Amy's small act of kindness ripples further than either of them could imagine. The Polish Donut is a warm, character-driven story about memory, mercy, and how even the smallest moments can sweeten a life.

ABOUT THE AUTHOR

Andy Labis

Andy Labis writes heartwarming, quietly surprising short stories about ordinary moments that change everything for people like Ben and the strangers Ben meets. His fiction lingers in the small details—a walk at lunch, a cup of coffee, a shared ride—that reveal how connection, kindness, and paying attention can reshape a life.

Drawing on a love of photography and nature, Andy brings a visual, grounded sensibility to his storytelling, often setting scenes along Midwestern paths, city streets, and in everyday neighborhoods. When he's not writing, he's usually behind a camera, out on a trail, or planning a new adventure, collecting the real-life textures that find their way into his work.

To learn more about Andy and his latest stories, visit:
www.allthingsandy.com
For more adventures in the "What Ben Didn't Know" world, visit:
www.whatbendidntknow.com

www.ingramcontent.com/pod-product-compliance
Lightning Source LLC
LaVergne TN
LVHW052301100826
845147LV00001B/115

* 9 7 9 8 9 9 4 5 0 8 2 6 8 *